I am a mammoth.

BAINTE DEN STOC

WITHDRAWN FROM
DÚN LAOGHAIRE-RATHDOWN COUNTY
LIBRARY STOCK

KT-174-594

I have big, thick legs. I can stamp on things.

I have long tusks. I can dig with them.

And I have a long trunk.

I can do lots of things with my trunk.

I can pick things up.

I can lift things.

I can drink.

I can slosh my mum and dad!

And I can smell things with my trunk.

I can smell *good* things...
Sniff, sniff! Bananas!

And I can smell *bad* things...
Sniff, sniff! A skunk!

This skunk stinks! I will slosh him!

Slosh! That will get rid of the smell.

Sniff, sniff...

Oh no! The skunk still smells of skunk.